THE COWBOY ABC

THE
COWBOY
ABC

CHRIS DEMAREST

A DK INK BOOK
DK PUBLISHING, INC.

DK Publishing, Inc.
95 Madison Avenue
New York, New York 10016

Visit us on the World Wide Web at http://www.dk.com

Library of Congress Cataloging-in-Publication Data
Demarest, Chris L.
The cowboy ABC / written and illustrated by Chris Demarest.—1st ed.
p. cm.
"A DK Ink book."
Summary: An alphabet book featuring words that are related to cowboys and their way of life, such as appaloosa and tumbleweed.
ISBN 0-7894-2509-2
1. Cowboys—West (U.S.)—Juvenile literature.   2. West (U.S.)—Social life and customs—Juvenile literature.   3. English language—Alphabet—Juvenile literature.
[1. Cowboys—West (U.S.)   2. West (U.S.)   3. Alphabet.]   I. Title.
F596.D43 1998   978—dc21   [E]   97-52630   CIP   AC

Book design by Liney Li
The illustrations for this book were painted in watercolor.
The text of this book is set in 18 point Cheltenham.

Printed and bound in U.S.A.

First Edition, 1999

10 9 8 7 6 5 4 3 2 1

For my mother,

who has the coolest

cowboy boots

 is for Appaloosa, a trusty steed.

B is for Buckaroo, who rides at top speed.

C are the Cattle that follow the trail.

 is the Dog, wagging his tail.

 is for Elk, majestic and fleet.

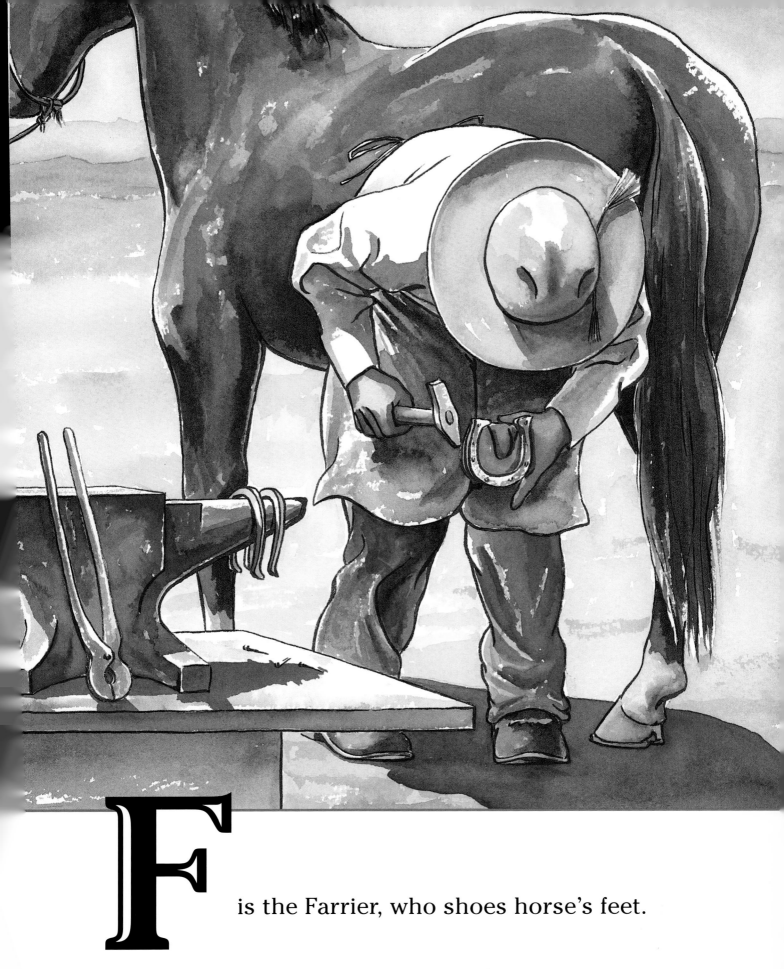

F is the Farrier, who shoes horse's feet.

G

is the Guitar strummed late at night.

 is the Hat that's pulled way down tight.

I is for Indian paintbrush in bloom.

J are the jinglebobs, jingling a tune.

K

is for Kerchief to keep dust away.

L

is the Lariat that brings back the stray.

M

is for Mesas that rise up so high.

are the Nighthawks that circle the sky.

O is the Oilcloth, slick when it rains.

P are the Prairie dogs; they live on the plains.

Q

is for Quirt—give a crack of that whip!

R is for Reins—Hang on tight! Let 'er rip!

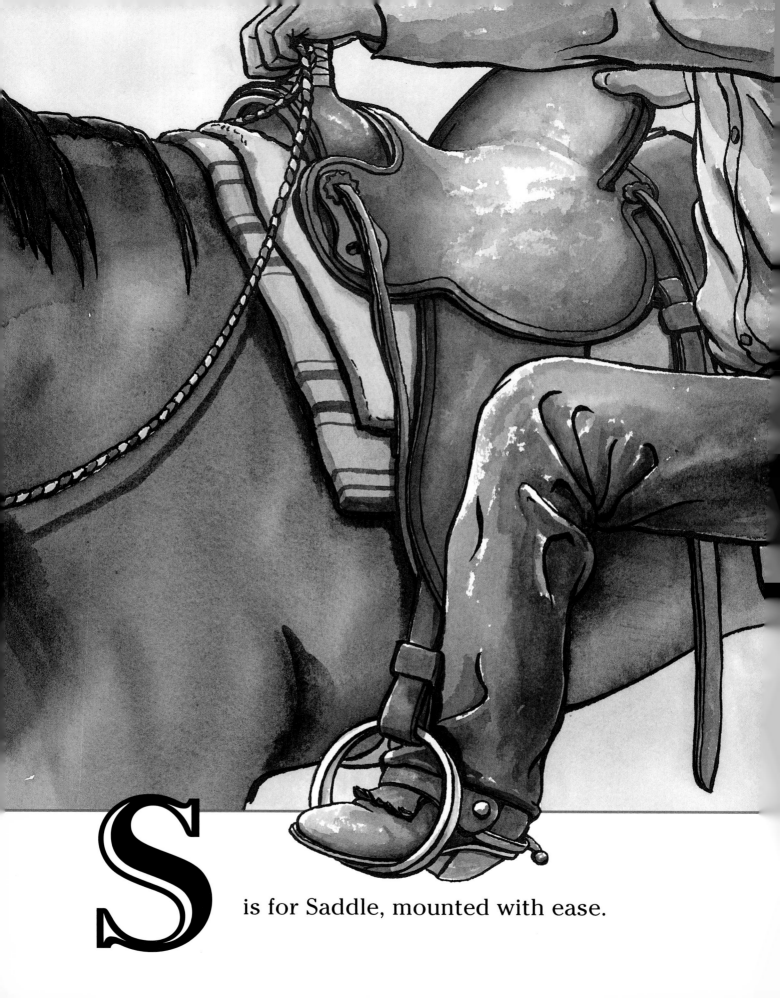

S is for Saddle, mounted with ease.

T is for Tumbleweed, tossed by the breeze.

U

's Union Pacific, its steam whistle sings.

V is for Vest that can hold many things.

W

's the Wagon where all meals are made.

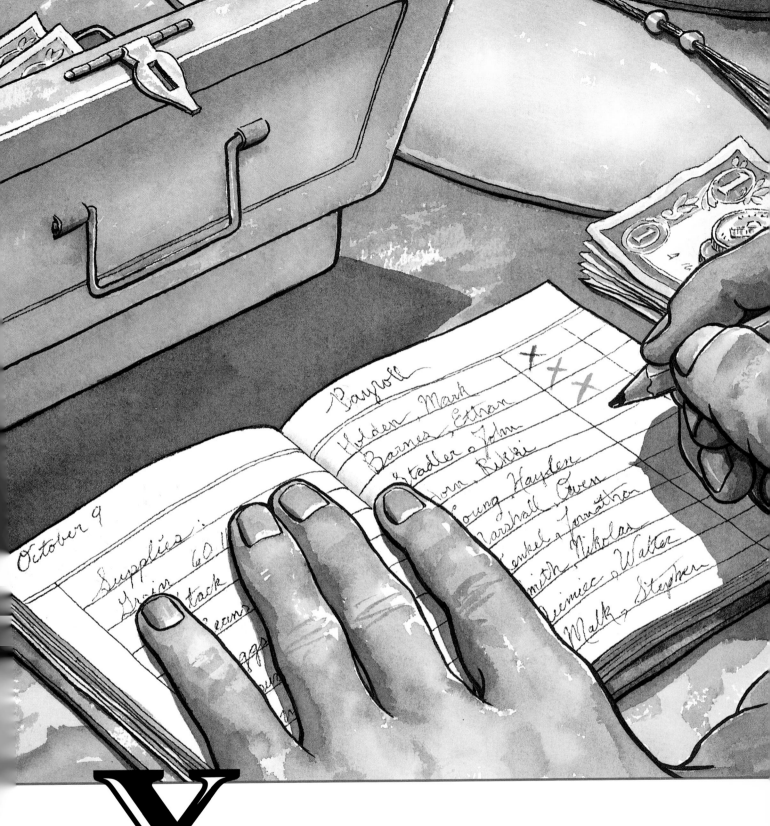

X

is the mark cowboys make to get paid.

Y is for Yearlings, by their mothers they stay.

 **Z** is the sound at the end of the day.

AUTHOR'S NOTE

If there's one thing the whole world identifies with the United States, it's the cowboy. In the 1950s and 60s, when I was growing up, the television screen thundered daily with the sound of hooves as the good guys caught the outlaws and peace was restored to the small frontier town. Ask your parents or even your grandparents about their favorite cowboy or cowgirl, and you'll hear names like Roy Rogers, Dale Evans, Gene Autry, Maverick, the Cisco Kid, Tom Mix, and the Lone Ranger. Though I lived in New England, a long way from the prairie, it was easy to imagine myself hopping on my favorite pony and galloping off to school. Of course I'd catch at least one outlaw on the way.

I wanted *The Cowboy ABC* to tell a story, just like the T.V. shows did. But, instead of a fantasy world full of heroes and bad guys, this book would tell of a different cowboy: the real hero who rides the long, dusty trail of a cattle drive.

The story of *The Cowboy ABC* starts with the appaloosa about to be saddled. Then the buckaroo hits the trail. My pictures show the many details that go into making a cattle drive successful: Dogs help keep the cattle bunched and moving. A farrier keeps the horses' feet healthy by replacing old or broken shoes. For cowboys riding drag (that is, at the rear of the herd), a kerchief is necessary to keep the dust kicked up by the cattle out of their faces. And though jinglebobs may not help deliver cattle to market, some cowboys love hearing the tinkling of the tiny bells as they walk or ride.

Today's cowboys appreciate the rich history of their jobs, and they continue many of the traditions and dress that have endured for more than a hundred years. In *The Cowboy ABC,* I tried to speak for them visually and show a bit of their lives to the rest of the world.

Chris Demarest